T0114953

The Crows Will Tell

A collection of *ngewa* – fables - from the Akamba of Kenya

Muli wa Kyendo

Published in the Ushanga Book Series in 2017 by the Syokimau
Cultural Centre, P.O Box 20257– 00100 Nairobi.

Series Editor: Emily Muli

Design: Mutua Muli

ISBN: 978-9966-7020-3-6

Other books by Muli wa Kyendo

Whispers:
"It's definitely a quick, engaging read with sympathetic protagonist. The story telling is very African in style."
— Samir Rawas Sarayji

The Woman of Nzaui: a play that dramatizes the role of women in African society.

The Surface Beneath: a novel about the life of African students in Germany.

Kioko and the Legend of the Plains:
"an incredible story with a tight plot, a character any reader will empathize with, and a wonderful lesson." — Megan Green

Contents

Introduction

In the foreword to his collection of African folktales entitled, *Nelson Mandela's Favourite African Folktales*, freedom hero and former South African President, Nelson Mandela writes, "It is my wish that the voice of the African story teller will never die, that all the children of the world may experience the wonder of African stories." My hope is that this collection of *ngewa* of the Akamba will contribute to the fulfilment of Mandela's wish.

The Akamba or Kamba of South Eastern Kenya would translate *ngewa* simply as "stories", although the more appropriate translation would be fables or parables or wisdom stories and legends. Parables, like those told by Jesus in the Bible, are distinguished from fables in that the characters are human beings. Fables on the

7

other hand have non-human characters - plants, animals, spirits, anything that can be imbued with human communication and characteristics. And both parables and fables are short. Going by these definitions, this collection is a mixture of fables and parables. The stories have both human and non-human characters. They also differ from this standard definition in that some, like "The Animal Village" are fairly long.

Unlike regular folktales which, in African context, were told to children in the evenings, *ngewa* are told at any time of the day. Men sat at the *thome* (an open fire place at the entrance of the homestead) where they told *ngewa* to each other and welcomed visitors with *ngewa*.

Ngewa (the plural and the singular are the same) are told among age mates and by older people to the younger ones, never the reverse. They are entertaining as in the story of *"Mwaka."* However, they remain focused essentially on the emotion that best brings out the lesson they are teaching as in the story of *"Owl and the elephant."*

I must point out that all the stories in this collection have been reworked by the author, although the essence of each is maintained.

The problems of translating African oral stories into English has been noted by many authors. The African traditional story depends heavily on a variety of techniques meant to intensify emotions, create drama, encourage audience participation, and create humour and comedy. A favourite technique is the use of repeated verbs as in the example: "He walked and walked and ran and ran..." Another common technique involves imitating the sounds of movements, as in the story of *Owl and the elephant*, "....they heard: *Ndu, Ndu, Ndu!*" The animals were coming!

Again as has been pointed out by many authors, fables and parables are the common heritage of African society. Communication would greatly suffer if

9

there were no parables and fables. Luckily, these stories have continued to evolve and change with time to fit new socio-cultural and economic circumstances. *"King'ei, the Thief"* provides a good example of this transformation as does *"Milk my cow"* or *"The animal village"*. They are clear testimony to the fact that the African story teller is not about to go silent as Mandela may have feared.

Ngewa remain the most effective way to get correctional messages across without creating defences. Persuasion and transmission of the society's moral values continue to be the key roles played by *ngewa*. The goal was, as it is today, to bring harmony, respect and concern for others.

Specifically, *ngewa* work to:

1. Encourage listeners to look inward. The question listeners should ask themselves is: Where do I see myself in this story? In this case *ngewa* influence attitude formation and behaviour.

2. Provide possible ways of handling situations. Here the question listeners ask themselves is: How can I apply the lessons in this story about human character to the situation I am in? In this case *ngewa* serve as a yardstick for moral judgement.

3. Transmit and reinforce the community moral values. By showing the virtuous being rewarded and the evil being punished they imbue the listeners with a sense of self-worth and purpose. Here the question is: Am I really living by the moral standards and values of the community?

Finally, the author has avoided appending morals to the stories in the belief that readers will draw out their own. Nevertheless, I would like to express my hope that the stories will stimulate your mind, upset your values and feed your soul. Then they will have done their part and contributed to the fulfilment of Mandela's wish.

-- Emily Keles-Muli, M.A

The Crows Will Tell

1

Kinyoowe and the animal tails

Long time ago, all the animals did not have tails. Then one day, the Creator decided to make tails for them. After he had made the tails, he sent them to the home of the grandmother of Kinyoowe, for all the animals to select for themselves.

When they got the message that the tails had been brought, the animals rushed to get theirs. Even those that lived far away

13

travelled long and tiring distances to reach the home of Kinyoowe's grandmother to get their tails. Every one of them wanted a good tail that suited their bodies and needs.

Some, like the hare, chose short and fat tails. Monkey chose a very long tail while the squirrel chose a bushy one. Pig chose a coiled tail and warthog and rhino chose stubby ones. After a long and busy period, all the animals had picked their tails from Kinyoowe's grandmother — all except Kinyoowe.

The other animals were surprised that Kinyoowe had not taken a tail. Some of his friends repeatedly asked him, "Kinyoowe, why haven't you taken a tail?" and others asked him, "Do you not need a tail?"

And to everyone who asked a question, Kinyoowe gave the same answer: "Why should I hurry? When I decide to get a tail, I will just walk over to Grandmother and get one."

Days went by and Kinyowe still didn't go to

choose a tail. Kinyoowe's friends eventually gave up pestering him to get a tail and left him alone.

One day, the animals decided to have a party. On the set date, they all came. The cat proudly strode in with his beautiful tail raised up creating perfect balance. Dog wagged his tail with joy. Zebra chased flies with his elegant tail while monkey hang on tree branches with his long tail....

Kinyoowe watched the animals, fascinated and delighted by the beauty and variety of their tails.

"I will be back in a moment. Just wait!" he told his friends as he dashed away. "Just wait, you will see what kind of tail I will come back with!"

Kinyoowe arrived at his grandmother's house panting. He hastily called out, "Grandmother, I have come to get my tail. Quickly give me a nice long one!"

Grandmother was surprised.

"You haven't picked one all these days?"

"No. It's now when I have come for mine," Kinyoowe said.

"All these days and I was giving away tails every day?"

"It is now that I have come for mine. Give me my tail and stop asking many questions. I need to get back to the party quickly or else I will miss the fun."

"Now my poor child: What shall I do? The last tail was taken only two days ago...."

"Grandmother, you know you are only joking and the party will end! Please give me my tail without wasting more time."

"My child, it's true I don't have any tail left. I gave out the last one two days ago. I am sorry you will have to live without a tail."

"But Grandmother I will be the only one without a tail!" Kinyoowe cried and cried but there was nothing Grandmother could do.

2

Owl and the elephant

Father Owl married a wife and took her to his home. Now, it happened that his nest was on a tree branch beside a path frequently used by elephants. Mother Owl was worried that the nest was not in a safe environment for her family. She feared that when the eggs were hatched, the babies would be trampled upon by the animals passing by. That was why she often pestered Father Owl to shift their nest.

17

"Let's move our home from here!" Mother Owl often urged. "Elephant and his family will trample on our children with their huge feet."

But Father Owl would ignore her pleas. "Elephant?" Father Owl constantly mocked. "What can he do to me?"

When the eggs hatched, Mother Owl's fears intensified. She kept her ears to the ground, her eyes constantly watching out for the huge animals.

One day, when Father Owl and Mother Owl were resting and preening on a branch next to their nest, and their new-born babies were learning to fly in the bushes, they heard: *Ndu, Ndu, Ndu!* The animals were coming! Terrified, Mother Owl looked up and saw a long line of animals approaching. And they were so many that the line stretched beyond where her eyes could see.

"Now the animals have come, what shall we do to save our children? I have been telling you all the time to shift the nest!" she cried out, flustering here and there frantically looking for her babies in the bushes.

"Just wait! You will see what I will do," Father Owl said calmly.

Finally, there was the trumpeting and then the heavy feet of elephants.

"Now the elephants are here! And it's only now that the babies are learning to fly! They will kill our children with their heavy feet! Do something to save the children, now!" Mother Owl cried, desperately.

"Just wait. You will see what I will do," Father Owl said.

"What are you going to do? You are just standing there doing nothing!"

As Mother Owl pleaded with Father Owl, the elephants arrived and trampled on their children, killing all of them.

"Now you have let our children die! You did nothing to save them." Mother Owl wept for her children.

"Didn't you see what I did?" Father Owl was surprised.

"What did you do? You just stood there watching the children die!"

"Didn't you see what I did?" Father Owl repeated in amazement. "Didn't you see how I cut them down with my fiery eyes? Didn't you see how I ruffled my feathers, puffed and glared at the elephants?"

Depressed Mother Owl entered the nest to mourn her children wondering, "What use is it to scowl at something instead of acting?"

3

King'ei the Thief

Long time ago, a young boy called King'ei and his friends ran away from school and fled to the big city where they had heard life was always fun.

In the big city, life was however, not as the boys had expected. There was no food and nowhere to sleep.

King'ei and his friends became street boys, helping motorists to find parking spaces and watching over the cars. The money they received was however, not enough for their needs and they started stealing. Within a short time stealing became their way of life.

One day the boys were arrested by the police when they were caught stealing. They were taken to court where they were sent to children's prison for several years.

It was when they were in prison that King'ei made a decision to stop stealing. He promised himself that he would never, ever steal again when he was released.

On his release King'ei returned home and started living the life of a law abiding young man. With the skills he had acquired from prison, he started a business which flourished. He build a nice house and married. His children grew up, went to school – and some even had their own families.

One day, however, King'ei was shocked when he heard a man refer to him as a thief. It was at the market where a tall, young man whom he had never seen before was giving directions to an elderly man.

"Do you know the house of King'ei, the thief?" the tall man was saying. "You take this road. Follow it until you reach a very large house – the house of King'ei, the thief. When you reach there, turn to your left and stop at the third house. You will have reached."

"All these years," King'ei wondered. "All these years and people still refer to me as King'ei the thief! It is long since I stopped stealing. I have reformed, raised a successful family....I have even helped people in need.... And people still refer to me as a thief. How long does it take to build a good name? Even if it was building a sky scrapper reaching heaven, would I not have long finished?"

4

The crows will tell

There was famine in the country. And two friends, Musyimi and Mwangangi, decided to go hunting. They prepared themselves, making sure that they carried enough arrows so that they would not return home empty-handed.

Because of the drought in the land, animals had gone farther away into the bushes, searching for grass and water. Musyimi and

Mwangangi had therefore to travel deeper and deeper into the forest searching for the animals.

After a whole morning of searching, the young men had little water left. They had little food left, too. Darkness was setting in and they were getting desperate when suddenly they spotted an antelope. They both shot at it killing it instantly. They then made a fire and roasted some of the meat.

Now it was time to divide the meat to carry home. Musyimi insisted that it was his arrow that had killed the antelope. He therefore wanted more meat.

Mwangangi, however, argued that they should divide the meat equally because that was the agreement they had made when they set out to hunt together as friends.

"I cannot agree to that!" Musyimi asserted. "I can in fact, take all the meat because it was my arrow that killed the antelope."

"I will not allow you to do that because it is

not fair," Mwangangi persisted.

The two friends were soon quarrelling heatedly.

"I can even kill you and take all the meat!" Musyimi who was now very furious threatened.

"You can kill me?"

"Yes! I can kill you in this deep forest and no one will ever know!"

"You can kill me! The crows are watching. The crows will tell!"

Infuriated, Musyimi shot his friend dead and carried all the meat to his family.

Mwangangi's family waited for him for days. Eventually, they sent search parties to look for him. Days turned into weeks and weeks into months and months into years and still there was no word about him. At last the villagers gave up the search and lost hope of ever finding him.

One day however, after many, many years, Musyimi was sitting outside his house with friends when a flight of crows perched on the fence. It reminded Musyimi of the words of Mwangangi.

"Do you know something, my friends?" he asked to gain the friends' attention. They all turned to look at him, waiting to hear what he had to say.

"Those crows remind me of something, my friends. Years ago, I went to hunt with Mwangangi and we quarrelled over the antelope we had killed. I shot him dead. But before I killed him, he told me that even if I killed him in that deep forest the crows were watching. He told me, 'The crows will tell.'

"It's now many, many years since I killed him and I have waited for the crows to tell, but up to now, my friends, not a single crow has come to tell on me!"

5

Mwaka

Ngwata and Makwata were two very close friends. They frequently visited each other.

Now it happened that it was Makwata's turn to visit his friend. It was however the time for harvest and Makwata was very busy in the farm. So he decided to send his son, Mwaka, to see how his friend was doing.

Ngwata was overjoyed to see his friend's

son. He welcomed him with much enthusiasm.

First he gave him milk in a gourd. Mwaka took the gourd and drank the milk. Although he noticed that the milk had flies, Mwaka drank it because he thought it was customary for his host to welcome visitors with milk that had flies in it.

After a while however, Ngwata noticed that the milk the boy was drinking had flies. He was shocked and confused, wondering what his friend would think of him when he learnt that he had fed his son with milk which had flies.

"I must do something quickly!" Ngwata thought. But what could he do that could erase the mistake he had made?

After a moment of thinking, an idea came to him. "Mwaka," he called out to the boy, quickly taking the gourd away.

"Come I show you something," he said, leading him by the hand. "You know you are the son of my greatest friend?"

"Yes," Mwaka answered respectfully.

"Because of that I want you to really enjoy yourself. I have decided you should not return home so quickly. Stay and have some fun!

"Tomorrow, we shall slaughter that goat for you so that you can enjoy yourself before you go home," he said, pointing at a fat goat.

Mwaka was delighted.

The next day, the goat was slaughtered and Mwaka was given the juiciest parts. Ngwata made sure that he pointed out to the boy that he was giving him the best parts of the meat.

The next day, Ngwata called Mwaka. "Now you can go home tomorrow. You have been a very nice boy. But now, my little boy, tell me: What will you tell your father when you reach home?"

"I will tell him what a nice man you are!"

Mwaka started without hesitation. "I will tell him you welcomed me very well. First you gave me a big gourd full of milk and flies which I took. Then you slaughtered a goat for me and gave me the best parts."

Ngwata was disappointed that the boy was still remembering the milk with flies. *"What can I do for this boy to forget about the flies?"* He wondered.

"I have changed my mind," Ngwata told the boy suddenly. "I just remembered there is something else I haven't done. So you will not go home tomorrow because I will call all the villagers to come and say goodbye to you in a big party."

The next day Ngwata called all the villagers. There was a big party. A bull was slaughtered. There was feasting, song and dance. Mwaka and the other children enjoyed themselves greatly.

After the party, Ngwata called Mwaka. "Now you will go home tomorrow. But now, my little boy, tell me: What will you tell your father when you reach home?"

"I will tell him what a nice man you are. First you welcomed me with milk full of flies. After I had drank the milk you slaughtered a goat and gave me the best parts. Then the next day, you put a big party for me in which you slaughtered a bull. It was great fun for me and the children."

Ngwata was lost for words. He had run out of options and decided to let the boy go home.

6

Frog's golden silence

Frogs and snakes lived near each other. And although they shared the lake where they went for hunting, they were not friends. The frogs went to hunt insects while snakes went to hunt frogs.

One day, the snakes went to the lake as usual but they did not find frogs to catch. The lake was wide and the frogs had gone to another side of it to hunt for insects. The

33

snakes waited for the frogs and eventually went home hungry and disappointed.

It was however a successful hunt for the frogs as they had caught many insects. Even Baby Frog had carried home some insects.

It was night time when the frogs arrived back home and they realized they didn't have fire to cook. As they were wondering what to do, Baby Frog saw a house which had light.

"Mother, look there is a house with fire over there!" Baby Frog said excitedly.

"Yes, dear, I can see that, too. They could help us with live coals to start ours," Mother Frog said. "Get into the house and wait for me. I will go over there and get some coals."

Mother Frog hopped into the darkness and soon she stood at the door of the house where they had seen a light. The house was pitch dark except for a flicker of light but nevertheless, Mother Frog knocked at the door.

"*Hodi*!" Mother Frog called out as she stood at the door.

"Welcome!" a voice answered from the inside but no one came out to open the door.

"May I have some fire?"

"No," the voice said. "We are just trying to light ours. You see we spent the whole day at the lake hunting for frogs."

"Did you get any?"

"No, we didn't. Not even a single frog came to the lake today."

Quietly, Mother Frog retreated thinking to herself, "It's good I was slow to speak. If I had revealed myself as a frog, I would have been Snake's supper tonight!"

7

Birds of fortune

Two young men, Muoka and Kioko, set out in search of wealth. Muoka was very poor and had not prepared any food for the journey. Kioko had however packed a lot of food.

They started their journey early in the morning and walked and walked the whole day long. They climbed hills and crossed valleys. The sun was burning hot and the young men became very tired and hungry. They had already reached the plains when darkness set in. They settled under an acacia tree for the night. Kioko took out his food and started to eat. Muoka who had no food hungrily watched his companion eat. He had hoped that Kioko would share some food with him, but he didn't.

Early in the morning, they continued on their journey. Although Muoka was very hungry, he tried as much as he could to keep pace with his friend.

After many days of walking and staying without food, Muoka became so weak that he could not resist the temptation to ask his companion for some food. Kioko however, told him: "Let me take out your eye and I will give you some."

Muoka was so hungry that he agreed. Kioko took off Muoka's eye and gave him some food which was too little to satisfy.

On and on they walked. The sun set and they still walked on. When they became too tired

37

to walk any farther, they found a comfortable place by the wayside and slept on the grass.

Muoka who could now see with only one eye, begged his friend for a bit of food, but Kioko refused.

Muoka was so hungry and thirsty that his lips were very dry. He tried to moisten them by passing his tongue over them but the tongue was also very dry.

In despair, Muoka took a piece of stick and hit the ground as he sang, the way he had heard that people in the plains did:

Earth open,
Earth open.

At last a lump of soil popped up and clean and fresh water gushed out. Muoka drank and drank until he was satisfied.

Kioko, who was also very thirsty, pleaded: "Let me drink some also."

When Muoka refused, Kioko told him, "If

you let me drink, I will give you some food."
Muoka allowed Kioko to take the water and
in return Kioko gave him a very small
amount of food.

The young men continued their journey.
They travelled for many days and again
they became hungry. Muoka again begged
Kioko for some food.

Kioko replied, "I will give you some if you let
me take out your other eye." Because he
was emaciated, Muoka agreed. Kioko took
out Muoka's eye, then he put a little food
beside him and continued on the journey
alone.

As Muoka was now blind, he could not see
the food. He groped for it but he could not
get it. Eventually he decided to move on
feeling his way with his hands until he came
to a tree with a good shade. He lay there
wondering what to do next.

He hadn't been there for long however,
when a noisy flight of birds patched on the
tree. One of the birds said:

"O, men, if the bush had no ears I would tell you something."

The others chorused: "Tell us!"

The bird said, "If you take a small stick from this tree and you hit a mad man with it, he will be cured."

The birds then flew away.

A short while later, another flight of birds came and perched on the tree. One bird said, "O, men, if the bush had no ears, I would tell you something".

The others chorused: "Tell us!"

The bird said, "If you take a leaf from this tree and you rub it on a blind man, he will regain his sight."

The birds then flew away.

Muoka groped for a leaf from the tree and rubbed it on the sockets of his eyes. And to his surprise he could see again! He was elated. He cut a stick from the tree and started his journey again.

He walked until he reached another country. He was told that the ruler of that country allowed people to enter his country only if they were able to cure madness.

Muoka immediately said, "I can cure it!"

Now it happened that the ruler of that country had a daughter who was mad. He told Muoka, "Whoever will cure my daughter, I will give him my daughter and my country, too."

The girl was brought to Muoka. He took out the piece of stick that he had and hit the girl with it. Suddenly the girl told her mother, who was present, "Mummy give me a basket, I want to go and pick fruits at the garden!" She went to the fruit garden and came back with a basket full of fruits. She was no longer mad.

Muoka married the girl and became the ruler of the country.

Days turned into months, and then, one day, Kioko heard that Muoka had become very wealthy. He went to see him and was very impressed and full of envy. He, too, wanted to be a rich ruler of a country. So he asked Muoka, "How did you come by so much wealth, my friend?"

Muoka told him of the troubles he had gone through when he, Kioko, left him blind and hungry and how the birds had helped him.

Kioko who was listening keenly said, "I will go there, so I too, may become wealthy."

Kioko immediately set out for the place where the tree was and sat there to await the birds of fortune. Flights of birds came and passed without perching on the tree. At last one flight settled on the tree and one bird said, "O, men, if the bush had no ears I would tell you something."

Excited that he was now going to become very wealthy, Kioko answered the birds at the top of his voice, "Tell us!" But the birds knew that there was someone listening and they flew away.

Kioko waited and waited hoping that another flight of birds would come. He waited until he was emaciated but none came.

8

Mwati

Once upon a time there was a man whose name was Mwati. He had a feather on his head which had been there since the day of his birth. This feather helped him in many ways - in getting cattle, goats, sheep, fame - and especially when he was in trouble.

His neighbour was however, envious and wanted to steal Mwati's feather. His eyes were always open for a chance to pluck out the feather.

One day, the envious man followed Mwati to a beer drinking party. All the people at the party, including Mwati, drank so much that they soon fell asleep. The envious man however, did not sleep. He had drank very little beer because he spent his time carefully watching and planning how to take away the feather.

When he was sure that Mwati was in a drunken sleep, Mwangangi, for that was the envious man's name, gently pulled out the feather and escaped with it. Mwati woke up to find his feather was gone. He was distressed and cursed whoever had stolen his feather.

Mwangangi went home elated that he now had the feather he always wanted. With the feather he would from now on get all the good things that he had dreamed of— goats, cattle and fame—just like Mwati had.

At home he was however, shocked to find his wives and his children were all gone. His one goat had died and his granaries were also empty. The feather had brought him great misfortune instead of all the good things he had expected. What was he to do, now?

Mwangangi sought help from the elders who advised him to slaughter a fat sheep, take its fat, pour it into the hole in Mwati's head and return the feather to its position.

Mwangangi did as he was told and set out to look for Mwati. It was not easy to find him for without the feather, Mwati had become a restless wanderer — always moving aimlessly from village to village.

Mwangangi searched far and wide. He walked everywhere asking the people he met if they had seen Mwati. He walked for so long that his feet became sore.

After many days, Mwangangi was able to pick up Mwati's trail. A group of men told him: "We saw him during the last rain season!" He was so excited he started to sing as he walked hoping that Mwati would hear him and come for his feather:

Mwati, Mwati, Mwati,
Come for your feather Mwati,
All my people have left me, Mwati,
It is only you who can help me, Mwati.

He walked and walked, and ran and ran, and whenever he met someone, he asked: "Have you seen Mwati?"

Some old men told him: "We saw him during the moon that past."

He continued walking and running, following the path he was told that Mwati had taken.

In one village he was told, "Mwati asked for water here a few days ago." His hopes of reaching Mwati were increased.

"Have you seen Mwati?" he asked in another village.

"He ate with us here four days ago", he was told. And yet at another he was told, "He rested here the day before yesterday,"

He walked and walked and ran and ran until he reached a village where he was told: "Mwati passed here this morning."

Mwangangi ran faster and faster and sang louder and louder. He was seeing an end to his troubles.

An old man who was grazing cattle told him, "Mwati has just passed here."

Then to his greatest joy, he saw Mwati sleeping under a tree. Carefully, he made his way to where he was, quickly poured the sheep's oil into the hole in Mwati's head and stuck the feather back. Mwangangi was so relieved that he ran back home without stopping.

At home, he was comforted to find all his belongings - his wives, children and goat had come back. Everything was just like it had been before he took the feather.

9

Mbuambui

Mbuambui, the spider, was tired of weaving webs. It seemed to him the work never ended. And besides, it took a lot of energy including watching for insects that were caught up in the web. The insects were the food for the spiders.

To catch insects, Mbuambui had to constantly make fresh sticky webs which, within a short time, became useless cobwebs. Making new webs was a laborious task for a tiny creature like a spider,

49

Mbuambui thought.

That was the reason why he decided to learn alternative ways of catching insects from the Creator. He knew the Creator, the one who possesses all wisdom, lived high up in the hills. But Mbuambui was willing to travel the journey, if it could save him the labour of weaving cobwebs.

Mbuambui set a day to start his journey. He started preparing himself as well. He saved many insects for food on his journey. And on the appointed day, he woke up very early. By the time the sun was up, Mbuambui was standing at the foot of a very tall, steep hill which stood next to another one which was equally tall and steep.

"I have come to see the Creator, the one who owns all the wisdom. Where does he live?" Mbuambui asked Elephant whom he found stuffing his huge mouth with large tree branches at the base of the hill.

Elephant sized him up.

"Take this path," Elephant said helpfully, "follow it until you reach the tip of the hill. There you will find the Creator, the one who holds all wisdom."

"Thank you very much," Mbuambui was very grateful to Elephant. He was glad, too, that he was near the Creator, the wise one. He thanked Elephant profusely and started to climb the hill.

He took the path that Elephant had pointed out to him.

By the second day, Mbuambui had already run short of food yet he had walked only a short distance from the base of the tall hill. He had to rest and make a web to catch more insects. Unfortunately, it was a rocky part of the hill and there was no grass and therefore, hardly any insects.

Mbuambui was wondering what to do when Lizard slithered out of nowhere. Mbuambui dived into a crack from where he watched the movement of Lizard. Lizard looked this way and that way before he repeatedly hit the rock with his head. Then he dashed towards Mbuambui who pressed against the rock, farther into the crack. He was shaking with fear when, to his amazement and relief, Lizard fled past as if he was being chased by a powerful animal.

Mbuambui stayed hidden in the crack for a very long time before he got courage to creep out. Slowly and carefully he came out, looking this way and that way to see if Lizard had gone away.

It was after many months of climbing and many more such dangers that Mbuambui finally reached the highest peak of the hill.

"I have come to see the Creator, the owner of all wisdom," Mbuambui told Lion who was taking a leisurely walk.

Without saying a word, Lion took Mbuambui to the side.

"You see the peak of that steep hill," Lion said, pointing at the hill across. That snowy peak is where the one you are seeking lives."

Mbuambui noticed that the hills were joined by a thread as thin as a strand of a spider's web. He looked down. He was so high up that the huge river that flowed between the hills was like a thin thread below.

He felt dizzy staring. "What if he fell down walking over the thin thread?" Mbuambui wondered. He felt cold water running down his body at the thought.

"If that is where the Creator lives," Mbuambui thought, "I'd rather go home. I no longer need His wisdom," he said as he climbed down the hill, abandoning his search.

10

The animal village

It was early in the morning in the Animal Village when Elephant woke up to find his wife killed and her tusks removed. "This is the work of Man!" Elephant cried out. His loud trumpet sound brought all the animals to his home.

Leopard was the first to arrive. He saw the tragedy that had befallen Elephant. He promised Elephant that the animals would do everything they could to ensure that Man did not trouble them again.

With speed, Leopard moved from house to house calling all the animals to a meeting. He went to the house of his friend and cousin Lion, to the house of Hyena, to the house of Hare, to the house of Hippopotamus and even to the houses of the small Squirrel and crawling Snake. "You must all attend the meeting!" Leopard announced.

On the appointed day, all the animals assembled under the huge, umbrella-shaped acacia tree near the Hippo Pool. Big animals like Elephant, Lion, Buffalo and Rhinoceros sat in the front row under the shade together with Leopard. Hippopotamus stayed at the edge of the pool to keep himself cool. Small animals sat in the hot sun or up in the tree. Their determination to free themselves from Man was so great that they didn't feel the heat of the scorching midday sun.

Leopard was the first to speak. He welcomed Elephant to describe yet again, what had happened. And Elephant's painful description of how Man had killed his wife because of her tusks moved the animals so much that many of them cried aloud and stomped on the ground.

Hare shot up from the crowd.

"For these and many more reasons, we must get rid of Man if we are to live peacefully in this wonderful village that God gave us!" he concluded his long speech. There was thunderous applause and cries of "Yes! Yes!" from the crowd.

"We must get rid of Man's oppression! We must stand together as animals and get rid of Man!" Leopard concurred.

The animals made an agreement that an attack on one animal by Man was going to be treated as an attack on all the animals of the Animal Village. "Unity is strength," they affirmed.

They elected a team to lead the fight against Man. Elephant and Leopard were chosen as the leaders.

United, the animals were so successful that within a short period they had vanquished Man and driven him away from their village. Man fled and went far, deep into the forests in the hills, cursing and promising himself to return someday.

Without Man the animals could at last live happily in their village. And the animals decided to keep their unity by establishing the Animal Village where every animal would be free – where every animal would be treated the same regardless of size, beauty, power, speed or numbers of their kin. The team that had so successfully led them against Man continued to lead them.

Elephant was however, a careless animal. Once he was freed from Man, he went his way, his huge feet hammering the ground so hard, the earth trembled. Behind him were his new wife and their children. When Leopard called a meeting, Elephant did not come. He was busy felling giant trees with his trunk and stuffing his mouth with tree branches.

The animals decided to replace Elephant. Leopard was the biggest supporter of Scavenging Hyena. Many animals, especially the crawling and non-carnivorous ones were not pleased with the selection of Hyena. With Leopard's position in leadership, the proposal to replace Elephant with Hyena couldn't be challenged.

"My fellow friends," Leopard said, "do not forget the reason we came together. Man is not far away from us!"

"That is true Leopard. We must work together!" scavenging Hyena added.

But without the fear of Man, the animals went back to their old ways. There were complaints of Leopard attacking other animals. Scavenging Hyena who benefited from the killings however, stood with Leopard.

The complaints however increased and spread, threatening peace and harmony in the Animal Village. There were calls for fresh leaders. Eventually Leopard and Hyena had to call a meeting. Many animals offered themselves for leadership. Snake was supported by all the crawling animals while Zebra was supported by all the non-carnivorous animals. The campaigns were so fierce that many unpleasant words were exchanged. In one campaign, Snake told the animals not to trust Hyena because "a hyena will always laugh like one even if he wears a sheep's cloth." This offended Hyena a great deal but Snake refused to apologize saying that what he had said was a well-known fact.

On the voting day, a large number of animals turned up to vote. Antelope came, fat and splendid in his beautiful, new clothes. He sat in front with Leopard and Hyena as they watched Porcupine with his body armed with prickles and Jackal with a long snout, entertaining the crowd with their antics before the election.

Soon, the crowd was large and thick. Leopard, Buffalo, and Bull, were among the fiercest critics of Elephant for not caring about animal unity and peace. When they finished they were warmly applauded. Antelope, with his enthusiasm for beauty, stood up to speak. He mocked Hippopotamus for his dreadful, massive body. "It looks as if it was badly cut out of your pattern with scissors by Mother Nature". Hyena, who undoubtedly was lying in wait for Antelope, went to be near him, pretending to admire him and throwing glances at him which did not mislead as to his intentions. Leopard was no longer paying attention. He was busy planning on how to catch Antelope who now stood so near to him their bodies almost touched.

At last, when he was not able to contain himself any longer, Leopard threw himself viciously onto Antelope, attempting to pull him out of the crowd so as to better strangle him. Antelope cried out desperately and Zebra, who was near, kicked and butted Leopard forcing him to release Antelope. Greedy, scavenging Hyena had already started to lick his lips. Confusion and panic filled the crowd. Leopard took the opportunity to attack Sheep who hopped about and butted Leopard. A heated battle broke out.

Lion tore an ear off Wildebeest who, in turn, gouged one of his eyes out. As the battle spread, many animals fled towards the forested hills calling out to Man for help. The predators hotly pursued.

Man grabbed his weapons and descended upon the animals. There were cries of attack, fierce fighting and shrieks of anguish. The Animal Village was in disarray with lifeless bodies of animals strewn all over the field.

11

Milk my cow!

Cattle were an important mark of wealth in Munyambu's village, but Munyambu had none. In fact, he and his wife were very poor.

One day while he was sitting outside on a stool, an idea occurred to him.

"I think I now know how I can get a cow and become rich," Munyambu excitedly told his wife who was busy sweeping the compound. "I will start by going to the forest to look for honey,"

"Mmm," the wife said with disinterest, as she went on with her sweeping.

"Then I will sell the honey."

"Mmm,"

"I know I will be rich and Fulani, that lazy man, will come to ask me for some money."

As Munyambu visualized how Fulani would come to beg him for money, he became very angry. "I can see him coming to ask me, 'Can you please give me some...."

At this thought, Munyambu shot up, his fists clenched as if he was in a fight. " I will not even let him finish. I will tell him: NO!." He hit the air with his fists, his emotions rising.

Then he continued, "Fulani will come to beg for my money and I will tell him: NO!" He was now so angry that he kicked the stool and it went rolling, scuttling the chickens.

Surprised, Munyambu's wife paused and straightened up to look at her husband. She watched, the broom still in her hand.

Munyambu picked up the stool and sat on it again.

"With the money I will get," he continued enthusiastically, "I will buy a fat cow..."

At the mention of the cow, Munyambu's wife put down the broom.

"Then I will milk it!" she exclaimed enthusiastically.

"Milk it! Whose cow will you milk! Milk my cow!"

A heated argument ensued.

"Yes! I will milk it! '

"Milk it! Whose cow will you milk! Milk my cow!" Munyambu was beside himself with anger.

"Yes! I will milk it – I will milk it a lot.'

Soon the shouts brought in the neighbours.

"She will never milk my cow!" Munyambu shouted.

One of the neighbours asked: "Where is the cow?"

12

Nzou and Kavaluku

There was great famine in the land because it had not rained for several years. To get food animals had to cross a wide and deep river to the side where there was plenty of food.

Kavaluku, the hare, could not cross the river and he sadly watched his family starve without food. Daily, he would weakly walk to the river and try to cross it, but it was impossible.

One day, Kavaluku, in desperation, decided to wake up and go to the river as he had heard that the river was calm at that time and he was desperate to get food for himself and his family which was starving. He woke up early in the morning and was already by the side of the river at dawn.

He tried to jump into the river, but he was afraid of drowning in the raging waters. Animals that could swim came, jumped in and swam away. Kavaluku was hungry and desperate. How would he ever tcross the river?

As he was pacing up and down confused and anxious, Nzou, the elephant, came along walking heavily mbuu, mbuu, mbuu. He was ready to cross the river.

Nzou noticed that Kavaluku was struggling to cross the river. "My friend," he called out to Kavaluku, "this is very deep river. Don't try to cross it like me - the elephant - because the water will sweep you away. Come, jump on my back!"

Nzou carried Kavaluku on his back and helped him to cross the river.

When they landed on the other side of the river, Kavaluku was full of joy and excitement to find all kinds of foods that he loved.

He ate and ate and ate some more until he could not walk. He sat to rest in the cool shade of a huge tree.

Nzou was also happily going about his work when an insect got into his huge nose. He jumped and stomped, but the troublesome insect would not come out.

In desperation, Nzou rushed to Kavaluku who was now comfortably sleeping on his back in the shade. "My friend!" he said, "My friend, please help to remove the insect in my nose!"

Kavaluku opened his right eye a little and closed it again. "My friend," Kavaluku told Nzou, "when I finish eating, I always take a nap. I cannot interrupt my sleep!"

Nzou pleaded with Kavaluku for help as he stomped on his large feet. "Please help me my friend!"

Kavaluku stared scornfully at Nzou. "You are acting as if there is anything which you have done for me. Carrying me on your back was nothing. You have done nothing for me!"

Nzou did not answer Kavaluku but continued to clear his large nose turning his trunk this way and that way. Suddenly the insect flew out.

Time came to go home. When they arrived at the river bank Kavaluku, hopped onto the back of Nzou with the food he had collected for his family.

The two started to cross the river and when they came to a point where the river was very deep, Nzou told Kavaluku: "When I reach here, my friend, I must dive to the river bed to cool my back?"

"No, no my friend!" Kavaluku pleaded

desperately, "My friend do not do that. My food will be swept off by the water. And I will be swept off, too! I don't know how to swim!"

"When I reach here, I must cool my back. The routine cannot be interrupted!" Nzou said, diving into the water.

13

Kithing 'iisyo and his son

Kithing'iisyo was well known for his devotion to carving. He liked to carve anything – people, animals and even trees. Because he didn't want disturbance, he had built his workshop high up a tree. Every morning he would wake up, take his tools and climb the tree to his workshop.

Without attention from his father his son, Kitai started stealing small things in the village. He would steal chickens and eat or sell the in the market.

Although the villagers complained to Kithing'iisyo about his son's behaviour, the father did not pay much attention.

One day, a neighbour caught him stealing his cow. The neighbour was very angry and took Kitai to the elders. The elders agreed on the day they would listen to the case and they invited Kitai's father, Kithing'iisyo as was the custom.

On the appointed day, the elders had their gathering and Kithing'iisyo came to listen, but because he was too devoted to carving, he carried along with him a carving he was working on.

The elders discussed. And Kithing'iisyo continued carving.

"Now we have decided," one elder announced. "We have decided we cannot let Kitai continue stealing from his neighbours. Our custom says, he must be killed.

However, the father has to consent, as is the custom."

They kept quiet, waiting for Kithing'iisyo to speak. But Kithing'iisyo was very busy carving. He had not followed the discussions at all.

"What do you have to say?" one elder eventually asked Kithing'iisyo.

"It is alright. I have nothing to say," Kithing'iisyo said without lifting his eyes from his work.

"The father says it's alright," another elder said firmly. " The judgement remains the same!"

The elders took Kitai away. One elder said, "Now that they have taken Kitai to be hanged, we can go home." It was then that Kithing'iisyo woke up to the reality of what was happening.

"Did I hear someone say Kitai will be hanged? You cannot kill my son!" He was frantically running in all directions. "Which way did they go?"

No one had however, noticed where the elders had taken Kitai.

14

The greedy Aimu

There once lived Aimu, the ogre, who killed and ate people. One day, Aimu saw a beautiful girl fetching fire wood. He captured her and put her in the huge bag which he always carried.

"Well, now that I have already eaten enough, I will carry this girl for my dinner later." And with that Aimu took his bag and started off on his way home.

He came upon a village where there were old men sitting outside at a fireplace. Aimu joined them and they told each other stories. When the men asked him what was in the bag, Aimu replied, "It's my treasure!"

He picked up his bag and continued on his way home.

After a long walk, Aimu came to another village and did the same thing. The people welcome him very well and sat down to participate in their stories.

Aimu told them stories about his wanderings and the villagers enjoyed listening to his stories.

But when they asked him what the bag contained, he gave them the same answer. "It's my treasure!" he told them. He picked up his huge bag and continued on his way home.

In the third village Aimu sat down and the people welcomed him very well. They fed him with a lot of food. Satisfied, Aimu decided to walk around and see if there were some fat people he could come to get another time.

When he was gone the people opened the bag, and to their surprise, they found it was their own child who was in the bag. They released her from the bag and in her place they put a huge stone.

When Aimu returned, he was surprised that the bag was much heavier. But not wanting to create much fuss that would make the villagers aware of what he was carrying, he picked the bag and continued his way home.

When he arrived home, Aimu ordered his clan of ogres to make a huge fire and roast the meat he had brought with him. They lit a huge fire with flames that blazed.

Being greedy, they were anxious to roast the meat.

"We should remove the meat from the bag and roast it directly in the fire," one ogre said, salivating.

"No, we should roast it in the bag. It will taste better that way!" another said.

In the end, the ogres agreed the meat would be tastier if roasted inside the bag. So they put the bag unopened in the fire and sat away to wait.

The stone became white with fire and Aimu and his friends thought it was fat. They couldn't wait to dig their huge teeth into it.

They were so greedy, they soon started arguing again among themselves about who would be the first to take a bite.

One very huge ogre was the greediest. He dug his teeth into the hot stone and suddenly the teeth peeled off. Without waiting, the others quickly followed suit and the same thing happened.

Finally, all the ogres had collapsed and died,

toothless, except for one who was blind in one eye.

He cut a branch and with it poked at the stone trying to examine what was wrong with the meat. When he found it was a red hot rock, he fled and he was the only ogre who survived.

15

The boy who swallowed a chameleon

Long time ago, people used to walk to the river to drink water. They would walk to the river, bend over it and scoop water with their hands to drink.

One day a boy went to the river and bent down to drink. Above him there was a branch of a tree that crossed over his head creating a reflection in the clear water. Now, it happened that there was a chameleon that was walking along the branch which the boy had not noticed. When he was drinking the water, he saw the chameleon in the reflection walking along the branch. Suddenly, it disappeared from the boy's view. The boy did not see how the chameleon disappeared so he believed he must have swallowed it.

Frightened, he walked to the village crying and vomiting, "I have swallowed a chameleon. I have swallowed a chameleon!"

The villagers rushed to assist him. "How did you swallow a chameleon?" the villagers asked him. He explained to them how he saw the chameleon walking in the water in the river and how he had swallowed it.

"Suddenly I couldn't see it. I must have swallowed it with the water I scooped!"

One of the villagers felt the boy's stomach. There was nothing unusual. "There is nothing in the stomach. You couldn't have swallowed a chameleon!" he told the boy. But the boy would not stop vomiting and crying out that he had swallowed a chameleon.

Unable to persuade or silence the boy, the villagers decided to go and see where and how the boy had swallowed the chameleon. They followed him to the river and the boy showed them where he had drank water with the chameleon.

On top of the branch, there surely was the chameleon walking. But even then, the villagers could not convince the boy that the chameleon was still on the branch – that he had not swallowed it. He continued wailing and vomiting.

"What shall we do?" the villagers asked each other.

Then they got an idea. "It is true, you have swallowed a chameleon. We shall get a medicine man to remove it!" they told the boy.

One old man went into the house and disguised himself as a medicine man. Then he put water in a calabash and came out with all the bravado of a medicine man. "Now, my little boy" he said to the boy putting the calabash of water before him. " I have come to remove the chameleon from your stomach. Now, cry out loudest and vomit! I am going to remove the chameleon!" The boy cried out loud and vomited. All the villagers shouted, "There is the chameleon! It has come out!"

The old man walked to the bushes and threw away the vomit. The boy now believed the chameleon had been removed. He stopped crying and vomiting.

16

Three cows and the lion

A long time ago, there were three very beautiful cows that lived together. These cows were sisters but had different colours. One was white, another was maroon and the third was black. The cows loved each other very much. Everywhere they went they were together. They were together when they went to the river to drink water and they were together when they went to the fields for grazing.

Now it happened that nearby, there lived a lion. The lion was very desperate to eat the cows. So he followed them wherever they went. He followed them when they went to the river to drink water and he followed them when they went to the fields to graze. Everywhere and every time, the lion was looking for a chance to attack the cows.

The cows tried to hide, but it seemed like the lion always knew where they went. Whenever they thought they had hidden from the lion the cows would suddenly be surprised to find the lion was next to them.

Since they stayed together, the cows always repulsed the lion when he tried to attack anyone of them. They would kick and chase the lion away.

"How can I catch them?" the lion always wondered.

One day, the lion called aside the white cow and the black cow and asked them, "You, my great friends – have you ever wondered how I find you everywhere you go?"

The cows listened keenly.

"Everywhere you go, I follow you. And I find you. You could hide away from me and I would never find you if you knew how I find you."

The cows listened with keen interest. They wanted to know because then they would not have to keep moving from place to place to hide away from the lion.

"Well, this is how I find you," said the lion. "You see your friend is maroon. That is blood. She goes leaving blood everywhere she goes. So all I have to do is follow the trail of blood. If she was not with you I would never find you."

The cows considered what the lion said. And although they loved their sister very much, they agreed that they needed to separate from her because she was making them visible to the lion and endangering their lives. The maroon cow was very sad and cried a lot when her sisters left her.

No sooner had they left than the lion pounced on the maroon cow which was now alone and powerless. He made a quick meal of it.

The white and the black cow thought they were now safe from the lion, but the lion still followed them. When they went to the river to drink water, the lion was there. When they went to the grazing fields, the lion was there. How was the lion still finding them? They wondered, although as long as they were two, the lion could not catch them. Every time he tried, they kicked and gored him and he fled away. But the lion was still desperate to eat them.

One day, the lion asked the black cow, "Have you ever wondered how I find you? If you go to the river, I am there! If you go to the grazing fields I am there also!"

The cow was interested to know. The lion continued, "It is because of the white cow. The white cow can be seen distances away. You black cow, you are so dark I cannot see you. Without the white cow, I would never find you."

The black cow considered what the lion said and decided to leave the white cow.

No sooner had the black cow left than the lion pounced on the white cow which was now alone and powerless. He made a quick meal of it.

Now only the black cow was left. And alone, she too, was easily seized and eaten by the lion.

Printed in the United States
By Bookmasters